Especially for Elliot Henry,
Ethan Charles, and Maverick Roy!
—A.S.C.

JF

I Can Read® and I Can Read Book® are trademarks of HarperCollins Publishers.

Biscuit and Friends: A Day at the Aquarium
Text copyright © 2023 by Alyssa Satin Capucilli.
Illustrations copyright © 2023 by Pat Schories.
All rights reserved. Printed in the United States of America.
No part of this book may be used or reproduced in any manner whatsoever without written permission except in the case of brief quotations embodied in critical articles and reviews. For information address HarperCollins Children's Books, a division of HarperCollins Publishers, 195 Broadway, New York, NY 10007.
www.icanread.com

Library of Congress Control Number: 2022933113
ISBN 978-0-06-291007-3 (trade bdg.) — ISBN 978-0-06-291006-6 (pbk.)

Book design by Marisa Rother

23 24 25 26 27 LB 10 9 8 7 6 5 4 3 2 1 ❖ First Edition

Biscuit
and Friends

A DAY AT THE AQUARIUM

story by ALYSSA SATIN CAPUCILLI
pictures by ROSE MARY BERLIN
in the style of PAT SCHORIES

HARPER
An Imprint of HarperCollinsPublishers

"Stay here, Biscuit.

We're going to the aquarium.

We'll see all kinds of fish,

and some sea turtles, too!

We'll be back soon!"

Biscuit watched the little girl

and her friends set out on their way.

Woof, woof!

Biscuit didn't want to wait!

Could he go along?

Woof!

Biscuit had never been

to the aquarium.

Which way could it be?

Biscuit sniffed here and there.

He passed the school and pond.

He passed the library and park.

Biscuit sniffed again and again,
until . . .

Woof, woof!

Biscuit found the aquarium at last!

He couldn't wait to go inside.

The aquarium was filled with fish
of every size and color!
Woof!

Biscuit saw sharks swimming by.

He saw tall tanks of jellyfish.

But it wasn't long before he found

what he was really looking for!

Woof, woof!

"Oh, Biscuit!

How did you find your way here?"

asked the little girl.

Woof, woof!

"Follow us now, Biscuit.
There's a lot to see
at the aquarium."
Woof, woof!

"Over here, Biscuit.

Let's stop at the touch pool."

Woof!

But Biscuit was not ready to stop.

He wanted to see the sea turtles.

The sea turtles wanted to see him, too!

Woof, woof!

19

Just then, Biscuit heard
a loud barking sound.
What could it be?
Woof!

Biscuit hurried past more fish.

He ran outside

and saw a crowd waiting.

The barking was getting closer!

Bark! Bark!

Woof, woof!

"Funny puppy," said the little girl.

"I knew you'd find the seals
and the sea lions!

Look! Here comes their trainer."

Woof, woof!

It was fun to see the trainer feed
the seals and the sea lions.
The seals swam gracefully
through the water.
The sea lions barked and barked.

Just then the trainer looked
here and there.
Was something missing?
Woof, woof!

Biscuit saw just what the trainer
was looking for.
He gave it to her at once.
Woof, woof!

"Thank you!" said the trainer.

"Seals and sea lions need

plenty of playtime!"

"A day at the aquarium
wouldn't be the same
without you, Biscuit,"
said the little girl.

"I'm glad you found your way.

I think we all are!"

Bark! Bark!

Woof, woof!